# WELCOME TO
# PASSPORT TO READING
### A beginning reader's ticket to a brand-new world!

Every book in this program is designed to build read-along and read-alone skills, level by level, through engaging and enriching stories. As the reader turns each page, he or she will become more confident with new vocabulary, sight words, and comprehension.

These PASSPORT TO READING levels will help you choose the perfect book for every reader.

**READING TOGETHER**
Read short words in simple sentence structures together to begin a reader's journey.

**READING OUT LOUD**
Encourage developing readers to sound out words in more complex stories with simple vocabulary.

**READING INDEPENDENTLY**
Newly independent readers gain confidence reading more complex sentences with higher word counts.

**READY TO READ MORE**
Readers prepare for chapter books with fewer illustrations and longer paragraphs.

This book features sight words from the educator-supported Dolch Sight Words List. This encourages the reader to recognize commonly used vocabulary words, increasing reading speed and fluency.

For more information, please visit passporttoreadingbooks.com.

## *Enjoy the journey!*

Little, Brown and Company

Hachette Book Group
237 Park Avenue, New York, NY 10017
Visit our website at www.lb-kids.com

Little, Brown and Company is a division of Hachette Book Group, Inc.
The Little, Brown name and logo are trademarks of Hachette Book Group, Inc.

The publisher is not responsible for websites (or their content)
that are not owned by the publisher.

First Edition: May 2013

ISBN 978-0-316-22829-9

Library of Congress Control Number: 2012942752

10 9 8 7 6 5 4 3 2

IM

Printed in Malaysia

Passport to Reading titles are leveled by independent reviewers
applying the standards developed by Irene Fountas and Gay Su Pinnell in *Matching Books to Readers: Using Leveled Books in Guided Reading*, Heinemann, 1999.

**LICENSED BY:**

# TRANSFORMERS® RESCUE BOTS

# Meet Chase the Police-Bot

*Adapted by* Lisa Shea

*Based on the episode*
*"Family of Heroes" written by*
Nicole Dubuc

**LITTLE, BROWN AND COMPANY**
New York  Boston

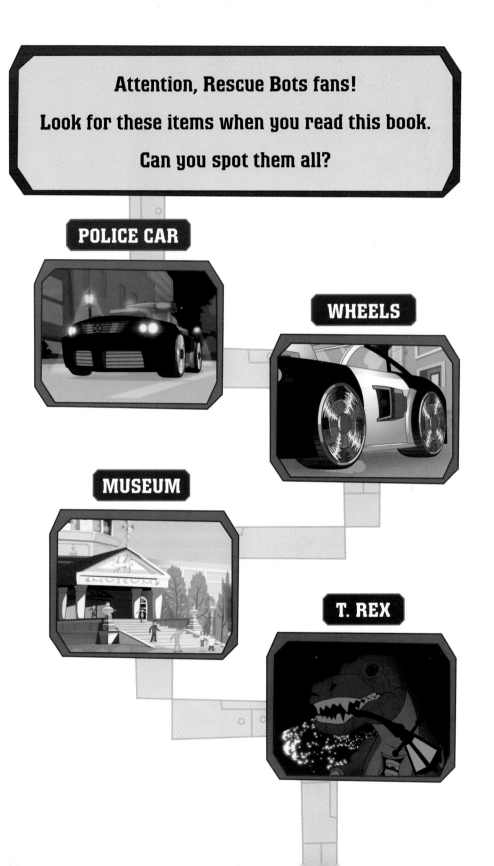

**Attention, Rescue Bots fans!**

**Look for these items when you read this book.**

**Can you spot them all?**

**POLICE CAR**

**WHEELS**

**MUSEUM**

**T. REX**

I am Chase the Police-Bot.

I am part of a special group

of Transformers

called the Rescue Bots.

Optimus Prime gave us a mission
to serve and protect humans.
The other Rescue Bots are named
Heatwave, Boulder, and Blades.

I can turn into a police car.

My lights flash when I blast my siren.

I am fast on wheels!

I have a human partner.

His name is Chief Burns.

I enjoy working with the chief.

We do not let anyone break the law!

Chief Burns gets an alert.
The museum is on fire!
It is time for the Rescue Bots
to go on our first mission!

The museum has old stuff inside.
Boulder goes in to look, but I do not.
Chief Burns asks me to make sure
all humans get out safely.

I do my job.

"Leave, please," I tell the humans.

"The museum is now closed."

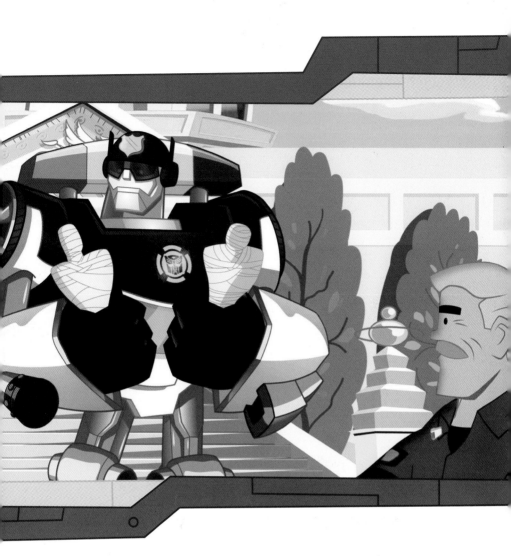

I am very polite, and I do not yell.

But two humans do not respond.

Chief Burns calls them mummies.

When the mummies do not move,
I arrest them!

Chief Burns tells me
that the mummies can stay.
"We do not need to worry
about them, partner," he says.

Inside the museum,
a dinosaur robot
is about to fall on a human!
The chief runs in to help.

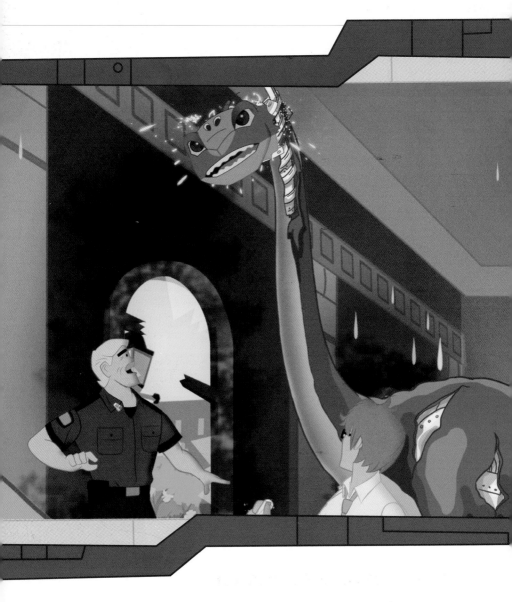

Heatwave is team leader
of the Rescue Bots.
He acts fast to catch the robot
and save both humans!

The Rescue Bots pretend
to be regular robots.
We are really alien life-forms.
Chief's family knows our secret.

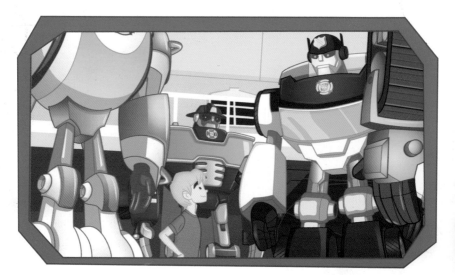

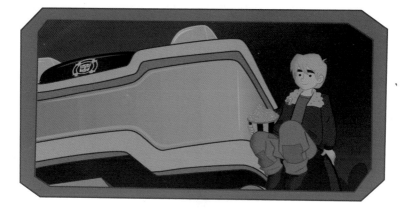

Chief Burns asks his son Cody
to help us hide in plain sight.
That night, Cody takes us to a movie
to learn about Earth.

Blades sees something and asks,

"Is that part of the show?"

There is a T. rex robot on the loose!

It came from the museum.

"The fire messed up the wires

inside the robot," says Cody.

"Chase, turn on your lights!"
Cody tells me.
I flash my red and blue lights
and play my siren, too.

The T. rex turns around
and runs to me.
That is what we want.
We want it to leave the humans alone.

"Now what?" I ask.

To keep people safe,

we agree to lead the T. rex robot

to a place that has no humans.

We change into our vehicles
and are on our way!
"Rescue Bots, roll to the rescue!"
says Heatwave.

Blades needs to get a cage.

To give him time to do that,

I race around with lights flashing.

That keeps the dino bot busy.

Next, we need the T. rex to sit down.

Heatwave knows what to do.

He waits for the right moment

and then slams the T. rex into the mud!

Blades is back!

He drops a metal cage on the T. rex.

Cody sneaks up and flips a switch.

He turns off the robot's power!

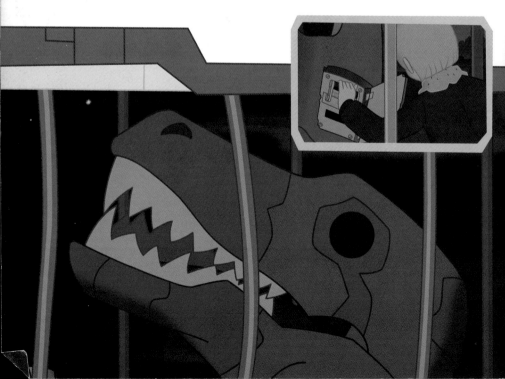

The chief is proud of Cody.

He puts him on the rescue team.

"I want a picture of all my heroes,"

he says as he takes a photo.

On the land, in the sky, or in the sea,
wherever there is an emergency,
there are the Rescue Bots!

Even if the emergency is just keeping humans cool on a hot day!

The Rescue Bots are always ready
to roll to the rescue!